For Elizabeth and Claire, who fill my
heart with joy each and every day.

# CHRISTMAS
# MOUSE
# Coloring Book

*Dedicated to Elizabeth, my inspiration.*
*Love you to the moon and back.*

Made in the USA
Las Vegas, NV
01 December 2024

13057417R00028